Antoinette
A Year in the Life of a Doll
with
Her Friends

Antoinette
A Year in the Life of a Doll
with
Her Friends

Stephanie C. Fox

Bloomfield, Connecticut, U.S.A.

Library of Congress Cataloging-in-Publication Data
Name: Fox, Stephanie C., author.
Title: Antoinette: A Year in the Life of a Doll with Her Friends / Stephanie C. Fox.
Description: Connecticut: QueenBeeBooks [2024].
Identifiers: ISBN 978-1-7343743-2-2 (paperback)
Subjects: 1. Fiction—Feminist. 2. Crafts & Hobbies—Dolls & Doll Clothing. 3. Political Science—Women in Politics.

www.queenbeeeedit.com

Cover design by Stephanie C. Fox
Photography by Stephanie C. Fox
Dolls and their clothes by Stephanie C. Fox
Printed in the United States of America

Other Books by Stephanie C. Fox:

Nae-Née — Birth Control: Infallible, with Nanites and
Convenience for All
Vaccine: The Cull — Nae-Née Wasn't Enough
New World Order Underwater — The Nae-Née Inventors
Strike Back

The Book of Thieves
The Bear Guarding the Beehive

Scheherazade Cat: The Story of a War Hero

An American Woman in Kuwait

Hawai'i — Stolen Paradise: A Travelogue
Hawai'i — Stolen Paradise: A Brief History

The Visitor Experience at the Mark Twain House

The Slamming Door: Bone Cancer, Asperger's, and Loss

Elephant's Kitchen — An Aspergirl's Study in Difference

Almost a Meal — A True Tale of Horror

*Dolls are the creations from our dreams.
We invent characters and stories with them.
We decide how they look, what they do, and
what matters to them.
They are us.*

This book is for people who care about the world.

For the purpose of this book, "the world" shall mean:

The health of the Earth's ecosystems, and…

*…a society that treats all living on the Earth —
humans, other creatures, and plants — with respect.*

For my mother.

The Dolls

Antoinette Frances de Sauvelle

This is Antoinette.

   Actually, her full name is Antoinette Frances de Sauvelle. She is a virtuoso concert violinist, a composer, a conductor, and a soprano opera singer who graduated from the Julliard School of Music in New York City. She also studied at the Curtis School of Music in Philadelphia, Pennsylvania.

Her violin was made by luthier Antonio Stradivarius in the 1680s.

Antoinette keeps smiling, ready to please her listeners. Because she is on the autism spectrum, she does not always make eye contact. Nevertheless, she makes sure to do that when she is done speaking, singing, or playing.

She has an extensive wardrobe, as her profession necessitates attention to sartorial details. Her couturière is happy to make her dresses and other outfits. Stephanie C. Fox designs and sews everything for Antoinette and her friends.

What does Antoinette want? Florals, nature themes, and other patterns that are relevant to her life as a musician. She is often annoyed by the dictates of the fashion industry, so she has declared her independence from it. Everything that she wears must have pockets. There is no chance that she will lock herself out of anything or any place, because she has pockets for her keys!

And…no one shall stop her from having beautiful floral patterns. As far as she is concerned, they are always in style. Her clothes are made from comfortable, soft, natural cotton. No ephemeral fast-fashion for her, to be worn and cast off. She invests in clothing that she will work in for years, which is better for the ecosystem.

Antoinette gives concerts around the United States, plus she appears in other nations. Her concerts often have a theme: herstory (women's history!), ecosystems and environmental protection, holidays, politics and current events.

Lilith Hermione Wandcraft

This is Lilith Hermione Wandcraft.

She is a witch, a lawyer, and a politician.
If she seems to have a concerned expression on
her face, she has good reasons for that: the state of

the world, both politically and ecologically, has plenty to be worried about.

Lilith works for the president of the United States, as a member of the Cabinet.

It's a secret post: Secretary of Magic.

She carries sensitive and top-secret documents that require a secure transport.

She also meets with her counterparts at state and local levels at home, and internationally.

Lilith enjoys her job because it gives her a chance to make a difference in the world.

She speaks at events that cover the same issues that her friend Antoinette plays her violin and sings for, and they often end up working the same ones.

The two of them are best friends. They met as students in New York City, and have kept in touch, planning more work efforts together ever since.

They enjoy sharing news of boyfriends, relatives, and friends.

They have also been lucky enough to meet a friend from out of this world…

Ileandra

This is Ileandra.

Don't ask me her middle or last name. They are too difficult for a human to pronounce, and she hasn't spelled either one for me.

Ileandra is an alien and a botanist. She is from a planet that is light-years away from Earth, elsewhere in our Milky Way galaxy. She has brought her environmental suit with her – her Small Gray suit.

Ileandra has huge eyes for a reason: she is nocturnal. She spends most of her waking hours at home working at night, because her planet's ecosystem is severely depleted. Millennia ago, its climate changed drastically due to overconsumption of resources, making most regions very hot.

Because that damage was inflicted millennia ago, by her people's ancestors, few plants and insects thrive there. Food is scarce. And it is too hot to work outside during the day. When a species functions at night, they end up with large eyes and better vision at that time than when it is lighter out.

Ileandra has traveled to our planet to collect samples of as many plants as she can, to take them home with her. She will then work to make them thrive in greenhouses and ultimately outside, in the ecosystem, so that her people will have more food to eat.

Botany is just one of many professions for her people, most of which aim to heal the damage to their planet. But it is what she does.

Antoinette found her outside, in the forest behind her back yard, and invited her to visit. She also introduced Ileandra to Lilith.

Follow her as she spends the warmer months of an Earth year with her friends, Antoinette and Lilith.

Follow Antoinette and her friends throughout a year!

January

New York Symphony Orchestra

Anti-Book-Banning Symposium

Evening to Rest and Relax

Evening with the BSO

Bird Lovers – Ornithophiles

Antoinette will be performing with the New York Symphony Orchestra at Carnegie Hall. They will be playing Ottorino Respighi's suite for small orchestra, "The Birds".

She will be wearing this chickadees dress for that concert. ❤️😃

If you would like to hear this music, it will play at this link:
https://archive.org/.../Dor%C3%A1ti+Conducts+Respighi/

She encourages you to look up any of the pieces that she plays and find out what they sound like for yourself. Most are easily findable on the internet.

20% off ALL hardcovers
THE
BELIEVERS
ZOE HELLER

Fighting Book-Banning

The free expression and sharing of ideas are vital to a democratic and civil society.

Lilith will be one of the panelists to speak in a symposium on book-banning at the famous Politics and Prose bookstore in Washington, D.C.

The participants will discuss the history of book-banning in America and elsewhere, and analyze the fear and emotional insecurity that leads to book-banning attempts. Examples from American history will be provided.

The event will include a session in which the panelists produce a list of books that have been banned. They will then open up the floor to the attendees, inviting them to expand the list. People will be invited to come up and write banned book titles on a large posterboard.

Evening to Relax Before the Next Concert

Antoinette has arrived at her hotel the night before her next concert.

After a lovely meal in the hotel's restaurant, she has retired for the night, because she has a busy day coming up. She will have breakfast in her room, then practice her concert program in her room in the morning, and then have lunch in the hotel café. After that, she will go directly to the concert venue to meet the members of the orchestra and its director, and do a rehearsal with them.

She must be full of energy for all of this.

It's great fun for her.

Evening with the BSO

Antoinette has a concert dress with treble clefs on black, with a matching, short-waisted jacket.

She is all set to play with the Boston Symphony Orchestra.

They will be playing Wolfgang Amadeus Mozart's Symphony No. 40 in G minor, K. 550 and Franz Joseph Haydn's Symphony No. 94 in G major (H. 1/94), which is more popularly known as the Surprise Symphony.

February

Year of the Dragon

Practice Makes Perfect!

Valentine's Day

Lilith's Plans

Bee Concert

Encore Bee Concert

Disney Music in Florida Concert

Dragons!

Antoinette will be playing at a White House dinner. It will be held on the evening of the Chinese New Year, and it is the Year of the Dragon.

She will play the movie score for *The Last Emperor* by Ryuichi Sakamoto first, followed by selections from Disney's *Mulan* by Jerry Goldsmith. After the intermission, she will perform the musical score from the movie *Crouching Tiger, Hidden Dragon* by Tan Dun.

The Chinese minister of commerce and the United States secretary of commerce will be the guests of honor at this event.

Trade issues will be discussed informally, to keep relations friendly between China and the United States, and to keep products coming from Taiwan.

Lilith will be there too, of course. They met at her house before leaving for the evening, and their boyfriends photographed them.

She and Antoinette are looking forward to eating Peking Duck, and dumplings for dinner, and tangyuang, which are glutinous sesame rice balls, nian gao, which are sticky rice cakes with red bean inside, and tanghulu, a crunchy candied fruit dessert on a stick. It has several different varieties of fruit shaped into balls on each long stick.

Practice, Practice, Practice...

Antoinette sleeps late, stays up late, and when she isn't giving a concert, she is planning the next one and practicing the music for it.

Her concerts are often for causes that evoke memories of human history and herstory, and for environmental protection and preservation.

It's a lot of travel, and even though she loves it, sometimes she just needs to catch up on sleep.

She has a lot planned, and she doesn't know what else may come up to disrupt or add to those plans, so she is getting some sleep while there is a lull.

Happy Valentine's Day!

Antoinette is dressed for a Valentine's Day concert at the Breakers mansion in Newport, Rhode Island.

She will play her violin, and she will sing some arias by Puccini – the ones that Dame Kiri Te Kanawa sang in the Merchant-Ivory movie *A Room With a View*: 'O mio babbino caro' from *Gianni Scicchi* and 'Chi il bel sogno di Doretta' from La Rondine (The Swallow).

After that, her boyfriend will meet her with a bouquet of red roses.

She has made Raspberry Linzer Heart Cookies to eat at home.

Lilith's Plans

Sometimes, Lilith slows down, rests at home for the evening, calls her boyfriend – or he calls her! – and she relaxes.

She's not very good at doing that, though, because she has so much on her mind, and so many things that she would like to accomplish.

Unfortunately, a lot of what she wants to achieve depends on the actions of other people, but that is the life of a politician. Nevertheless, she keeps at it.

Antoinette wonders how her friend copes with not knowing whether or not she will be able to make a positive difference in the world, or if her work will be undone later on by others.

That is the nature of politics in a democracy: one group comes to power and enacts and institutes changes, and then another succeeds it and may or may not leave them in place.

Bees!

Antoinette will be playing *Flight of the Bumblebee* by Nikolai Rimski-Korsakov at an event for environmental lobbyists and legislators.

It will be held at the John F. Kennedy Center for the Performing Arts in Washington, D.C.

Among the attendees will be the Secretary for the Environment.

Lilith will be there to network with the representatives of various ecological non-governmental organizations. They shall strategize ways to stop the use of insecticides in private yards, and go on to organize and promote methods of managing insect populations instead.

Orange Blossom Honey and Bees

Antoinette has the ideal gown for performing with the Orlando Philharmonic Orchestra at the Dr. Phillips Center for the Performing Arts, in Steinmetz Hall, in Florida. It has an orange and orange blossom with a honey bees' pattern in two hues, which contrast nicely.

The musical program will include the scores from such lesser-known Disney movies as *Mary Poppins*, *Escape to Witch Mountain*, *Freaky Friday*, *Pete's Dragon*, *Popeye*, *Something Wicked This Way Comes*, and *Flight of the Navigator*.

Orange cake will be served at the after-party.

March

Lobbying for the Environment

International Women's Day

Herstoric Interpreter

St. Patrick's Day

Twilight Tuesday: Organ Accompanist

State of the Union Address

Lobbying for the Environment

Lilith Hermione has a bumblebee gown in black and cream.

She will be attending a political event in it, aimed at stopping the use of insecticides and thus saving pollinators, including, but not limited to, bumblebees. Also attending the event will be politicians, environmentalists, lobbyists for insecticide manufacturers, and journalists.

Honey bees tend to get most of this sort of attention, but they are domesticated creatures. There are many other pollinators who need help, including bumblebees, other wild bees, and butterflies. Lilith will be pointing that out when she addresses the gathering.

Wish her luck in making a difference for the ecosystem!

Happy International Women's Day!

For International Women's Day on March 8th, Antoinette will be performing songs from the musical *Suffs* by Shaina Taub. It is about the fight by woman suffragists for the right to vote in the United States.

She will be doing this at the Ed Sullivan Theater, on *The Late Show with Stephen Colbert*, one of her couturière's favorite late-night comedians.

That fight began with the Declaration of Rights and Sentiments at the Seneca Falls, New York Women's Rights Convention, which ran from July 19-20, 1848. It ended in 1920 with the ratification of the 19th Amendment to the Constitution, granting women the right to vote.

Antoinette's dress is an all-white, herstorically accurate recreation of a 1910s suffragist dress. White was chosen as the color of the suffragists' dresses because it is the least expensive, thus enabling women of all economic backgrounds to participate.

Her sash, which says "Votes for Women," is bordered by other colors that were worn during that time, purple and gold.

Herstoric Interpreter

Lilith will be at another event that Antoinette will be performing at. It is to be held at the Women's Rights National Historical Park in Seneca Falls and Waterloo, New York.

Lilith has a Gilded Age gown in tonal purple with eyelet lace. She chose it because the fight for women's suffrage spanned roughly 80 years, including the 1880s. Historic interpreters sometimes dress according to the time that they are narrating, so she decided to enjoy that aspect of the job, too. In this case, since she is recounting women's history, she is a herstoric interpreter.

Lilith will be leading guests on tours of the home of the author of the Declaration of Rights and Sentiments, Elizabeth Cady Stanton.

Twilight Tuesday: Organ Accompanist

Antoinette will be performing *Adagio pour Violon et Orgue* by André Caplet, composed in 1868, with a professor from Trinity College, in its famous chapel.

The organ in that chapel presents concerts to honor its longest serving organist, Clarence Everett Watters, each year.

It is a highly sought instrument, played by expert organists from around the world.

After that, an orchestra made up of students from the University of Hartford will quietly take their seats. Along with Antoinette, they will play Aaron Copeland's *Symphony for Organ and Orchestra.*

State of the Union Address

Lilith is ready to attend the president's State of the Union Address.

Many women who are politicians wear white suits to this event to commemorate the suffragists.

Lilith's dress has a sash of white roses embroidered across it to evoke the sashes that the suffragists wore. It matches her suit jacket, which has a white rose embroidered onto each side.

Café Day – Free Time! A Rare Treat

Antoinette and Lilith have black cotton jersey pants with pockets and blouses/shirts to wear with comfortable black shoes. Sometimes, casual clothing is what's needed.

They're going to browse in some bookstores; they want to peruse the latest novels, biographies, political histories, and whatever else catches their attention on the shelves and tables. After that, the plan is to visit a café to eat cake and drink lattes. They saw a carrot raisin walnut cake in the case, and couldn't stop thinking about it.

April

Easter

Bird Concert

Alien Visitor

Cherry Blossoms

Earth Day:
Evening at the Isabella Stewart Gardner Museum

Happy Easter!

Lilith has booked Antoinette to play her violin outside the White House at the annual Easter Egg Roll event.

Antoinette will be playing *The Carnival of the Animals* by Camille Saint-Saëns on the lawn while the families enjoy the game and meet the president.

They have each made some Easter cakes to enjoy with their families later: Almond Butter Cake, Almond Cakelets with Pink Rosewater Frosting, and White Chocolate Cake with White Chocolate Frosting and Candied Violets.

Busy Day of Fun

Lilith has a lot to do.

Not only does she have to get Antoinette settled into her spot on the side of the lawn, but she also has to coordinate the Easter Egg Roll, liaise with the Secret Service to see that all guests are invitees and have been checked, and meet and greet everyone.

It's fun work, though.

She even gets to enjoy some of the desserts that are offered.

One point that she and Antoinette agree on:
The Easter Bunny is female.
She represents Ēostre, the Goddess of Spring.
Since when do boys have eggs?! They don't.

Birds!

Antoinette has a dress with a feathers-on-blue pattern.

She is ready to play for the Audubon Society, where an event to promote listing more bird species as threatened and endangered will be held. It is important to protect the birds from environmental threats with legislation.

She will play with a string quartet, because the piece is one of Franz Joseph Hadyn's String Quartets: Opus 33 No. 3 in C major, "The Bird".

After that, an orchestra will join her, and they will play Aaron Copeland's *Appalachian Spring*.

Surprise – A Visitor from Outer Space

Ileandra, a botanist from another solar system far across our Milky Way galaxy, has come to Earth to collect samples of our plants.

This is not her first visit; she was stranded here during the coronavirus pandemic. Now that it is over, she is back for a more open, overt visit in the hope that she can expand her repertoire of plants to take home and cultivate.

Ileandra is particularly interested in edible berries, so she is in luck: Antoinette and Lilith love raspberries, blackberries, blueberries, and strawberries.

Ileandra already knows about strawberries. That was the first berry plant that she found, and she fell in love with it immediately. In fact, she was found with an uprooted strawberry plant on her first visit, and had collected another one when Antoinette saw her and invited her to stay.

Her hosts will take her with them on their travels for the next several months, show her human life and culture, and provide the alien with plenty of opportunities to collect a wide variety of plants to take home.

The alien is flexible about what to look for, of course: she would like to consider whatever other plants her hosts introduce her to in addition to the ones she is thinking of.

Pajama Party!

Antoinette and Lilith are having a visit to plan events. Ileandra has been invited along. The alien botanist is looking forward to accompanying them on their travels, observing them as they work.

The Earth women will combine Antoinette's concerts with Lilith's legal and political work, making it all about saving the ecosystem, reproductive freedom, and international cooperation in outer space.

Their evening starts off with Antoinette's recipe for spicy dark hot chocolate, while she decides what violin pieces she will play and what songs she will sing.

Lilith will share some lavender tea later on as they figure out how to work those performances into her political networking plans.

Their pajamas are made out of cotton jersey fabric. Antoinette's depict pale pink roses. Lilith Hermione's depict juniper and blackberries on pale blue.

Ileandra's depict strawberries; thus far, of all of the edible plants she has collected and analyzed on Earth, it is her favorite. She is enjoying tasting chocolate as a hot drink, and intrigued with the chili pepper spice in it.

Her friends will show her how humans use spices in food, and get her some spice-producing plants to take home with her.

Cherry Blossoms

In 1912, the mayor of Tokyo, Japan, gave the United States a gift of 3,000 cherry trees. They were planted around the Tidal Basin in Washington, D.C., where they can be seen today, blossoming in gorgeous hues of pink and framing the Thomas Jefferson Memorial.

Recently, 140 of these trees were torn up during a restoration project, so Japan is giving the United States 250 more of these wonderful trees – the variety is called 'Somei-yoshino' – at a celebration event. The president has thanked the Japanese people, and will be attending the planting of the gifted cherry trees. Lilith and Antoinette will also be there, and they will bring Ileandra guest.

Antoinette will sing the Japanese song "Sakura Sakura" ("Cherry Blossoms Cherry Blossoms"), which has been popular since the Meiji Era (1868-1912), in English and in Japanese. Here are the lyrics:

Cherry blossoms, cherry blossoms,
In fields, mountains and villages
As far as the eye can see.
Is it mist, or clouds?
Fragrant in the rising sun.
Cherry blossoms, cherry blossoms,
Flowers in full bloom.

Cherry blossoms, cherry blossoms,
Across the spring sky,
As far as the eye can see.
Is it mist, or clouds?
Fragrant in the air.
Come now, come now,
Let's go and see them.

Plants for the Pure Pleasure of Them!

Ileandra is fascinated to see humans enjoying plants simply for their own sake. It is a sign of a sufficiently healthy ecosystem – or, at least, segments of the planet's biome that are healthy – that large areas can be devoted to this.

Her own planet lacks such areas. It was heavily depleted of resources and fertile growing soil during a time, now millennia ago, just after its own industrial age. Her planet is hot – so hot that it is too uncomfortable to work outside during the day. Food is grown indoors, in greenhouses, using nanobotic pollinators and a water purification and irrigation system.

Seeing how food grows on Earth is a treat for the alien, and she intends to work hard on her visit to collect as many nutritious plants as she can.

Seeing the cherry trees in bloom has made her think that it might also be nice – and okay with her people – if she brings a cutting home to grow there.

Her planet was once like ours, and her people long to be able to remediate the damage caused by their carelessly selfish, wasteful ancestors.

Fox Concert

Antoinette will play with the Chicago Symphony Orchestra. It is a special concert for children. They will perform the movie score of *Fantastic Mr. Fox* by Alexandre Desplat.

Actually, it's a bit more special than that, because it will be held at the Ann & Robert H. Lurie Children's Hospital, so that kids who are critically ill and unable to go out to a concert hall can have some fun.

The entire orchestra has agreed to go with her to the hospital for this event, and the hospital staff will bring as many patients as possible to the auditorium. Any kid who can't leave their room will still be able to hear the concert thanks to the hospital's local area network (LAN) computer system.

Sidenote: Antoinette loves foxes. Her couturière is amused by this, and she is happy to oblige her with outfits that show fox patterns.

Along for the Visit

Ileandra has come along for the visit to the children's hospital.

Antoinette asked her to come and see this, and added that even though there will be no chance to collect a plant on this trip, it was still worth experiencing. The alien agrees.

She saw how humans do their best to save critically ill children, and how many resources are poured into this effort.

It is depressing to know that if she were a doctor, she would be able to cure quite a few of them, but she is a botanist. And she is not supposed to be interfering anyway, so she's kind of relived that she lacks the ability to interfere in this way for that reason. Still…she wishes she had the ability, so she could break that rule.

The performance went off without a hitch of course, and the kids loved it. So did their parents and the hospital staff, many of whom were there to take it in and enjoy it with the children.

Earth Day:
Evening at the
Isabella Stewart Gardner Museum

It is Earth Day, and Antoinette will be playing *The Rite of Spring* by Igor Stravinsky in the courtyard of the Isabella Stewart Gardner Museum in Boston, Massachusetts. This space is a garden with a cathedral-glass ceiling. The theme of the event is self-explanatory: spring.

The museum guests will enjoy the music, the art in the museum, a brief lecture about the stolen art from the infamous heist of March 18, 1990, in which 13 works of art were taken. Among them were Johannes Vermeer's *The Concert* and Rembrandt van Rijn's *The Storm on the Sea of Galilee*.

The guests will also enjoy fine food and wine, followed by desserts.

A Lot to Think About...

Ileandra is happy to be visiting Earth, and to find out what it is like to live on a planet that is not too hot to go outside and breathe the fresh air and inhale the scents of the fruits and flowers.

It makes her sad that her own planet is in such a condition that her life's work as a remediation botanist matters so much.

At that same time, she feels incredibly lucky that this work has brought her here to experience all this.

She enjoyed wandering around the Isabella Stewart Gardner Museum very much, and was fascinated to see the children's hospital. Antoinette and Lilith are making every effort to show her a wide variety of places, plants, events, and issues.

All this thinking makes her tired. She hopes that the people of the Earth learn to appreciate what they have before it is too late, and their planet resembles her own.

She will get some rest in the pretty nightgown that Antoinette gave her and think about this more tomorrow.

May

Met Gala

Mother's Day

Concert in the Blue Room of the White House for Dr. Jill
Biden and Teachers

Concert at Colonial Williamsburg

Electric Vehicle Policy

World Bee Day – May 20th

Trip to Amsterdam and The Hague, Netherlands

Trip to the U.N. Office of Outer Space Affairs in Vienna,
Austria

Memorial Day

Met Gala

Each year on the first Monday of May, the Costume Institute Benefit is held at the Metropolitan Museum of Art in Manhattan, New York City.

Anna Wintour, the Editor-in-Chief of *Vogue* magazine, chairs the event and chooses its theme. The most recent theme was "Sleeping Beauties: Reawakening Fashion." (Everyone who attended stayed awake, of course!)

Antoinette wore a beautiful gown and figured that she had met the requirements of the fashion guru, who confirmed that by smiling as she gave the outfit a once-over glance and calling it "simply gorgeous".

It was a fun event for Antoinette: her boyfriend attended with her, and they met comedian Stephen Colbert and his wife Evie McGee, rock star Rihanna (who Antoinette complimented on her song "Sledgehammer" for the movie *Star Trek Beyond*), and politician Alexandria Ocasio-Cortez.

After dinner, everyone was free to walk around in the Anna Wintour Costume Center, which is a wing of the Metropolitan Museum of Art. The evening gave Antoinette's couturière inspiration for more of her creations.

Mother's Day

Antoinette loves to bake gourmet desserts.

She also loves to spoil her mother, who encouraged her throughout her education and into her illustrious career.

Therefore, she will play one of her mother's favorite things – tunes from the musical *A Chorus Line* – and serve her a delicious dessert of blueberry-lemon cake. Her mother loves lemon, so she will enjoy this cake.

Concert to Honor Teachers

Antoinette will be performing for First Lady Dr. Jill Biden, who, like herself, also wears gorgeously patterned dresses, at the White House, in the Blue Room.

Dr. Jill has some fruit patterns, such as lemons, and some floral patterns.

Antoinette can't get enough of berries, particularly red raspberries, but she also loves to have them mixed in with blueberries, blackberries, and strawberries. As for florals, irises, peonies, roses, and lavender are her favorites.

Today she is wearing a mixed berry pattern, because it includes blue.

The concert is to honor teachers, so she will play music from the movie *Mr. Holland's Opus*. She will donate her honorarium to the National Endowment for the Arts.

Tagging Along

Ileandra has been accompanying Antoinette on her concert tour.

She has met her hostess's parents, gotten friendly with her cat, and had a taste of many different human foods – in smoothies. Human food is good!

Well…on her own planet, there are good foods, too, but not while in transit to another planet. It's good to be eating fresh food again.

Antoinette lent her guest a blue dress to wear.

Her couturière is busy making more clothes for the alien, but they didn't have time to wait for them. The alien is not yet ready to out herself as an extra-terrestrial in public, but she plans to do so soon. Meanwhile, she is with Antoinette in the Blue Room of the White House, watching her play and holding her violin case.

Ileandra has introduced herself simply as a botanist, and then, fortunately, the concert began and people stopped chatting.

She joked to Antoinette that she didn't even have to ask to be taken to her leader, and Antoinette looked at her oddly.

"I follow human cartoons!" the alien told her.

Antoinette understood and burst out laughing.

Fortunately, they were walking down Pennsylvania Avenue, back to their hotel, when they had this conversation.

Electric Vehicle Policy

Lilith will be attending an event that addresses the CO_2 emissions caused by the fossil fuel industry, which really picked up steam (pun intended) during the age of the robber barons, which was during the mid to the late 19th century.

Ileandra's people went through an industrial age that inflicted the same damage on her planet. Because of this, she is very interested to go and watch what feels like a motor vehicle crash in progress as representatives of oil companies and car companies push for delay after delay on doing anything about transitioning transportation to electric power.

Privately, Lilith confided to Ileandra that all of this effort at cleaner vehicle emissions won't help if humans insist on maintaining their numbers at far more that the Earth can support, but that is an issue that, for now, she is forced to deal with separately. Far too few humans are willing to so much as contemplate it.

Ileandra's response to this was that by then, it will likely be too late to save the planet's ecosystem from the damage that such large numbers of humans are inflicting upon it.

There will be little left for future generations to live in…and on.

EVlinK
Schneider

Concert at Colonial Williamsburg

Antoinette has been invited to play at a reenactment ball at the Governor's Mansion in the historic town of Colonial Williamsburg, Virginia.

This is a living museum town. Everyone who lives and works in this fascinating place dresses as if it were still the late 18th century. Among the items worn there are ribbon hats. Antoinette is wearing the rosette style, which goes nicely with her gown. The gown even has pockets hidden under the patterned segments.

She will play dance music, including the standard *minuet*.

A tempting array of desserts will be set up at one end of the room:

Pear Tarts – Liberty Bar Cake – Almond Butter Cookies.

World Bee Day – May 20th

Antoinette has a dress with a pattern called Busy as a Bee Floral.

It depicts honey bees.

She will be performing for a group of melittologists – those are entomologists who focus on bees – at various places: Illinois, Kansas, England, and France.

The reason is that there are 4 different journals for melittologists, and they are located in those places:

1. The American Bee Journal in Hamilton, Illinois;

2. The Journal of Melittology at the University of Kansas;

3. The Journal of Apicultural Research in London, England;

4. Apidologie in Les Ulis, France (southwest Paris).

She has a lot of travel on her itinerary for the next couple of weeks!

Netherlands – A State Visit

Lilith will be visiting two cities in The Netherlands as Secretary of magic.

She is traveling with secure documents, entrusted by the president to deliver them. For this task, she has a dress with a navy-blue scroll pattern and lace. She will meet with the Chief Prosecutor of the International Court of Justice and the International Criminal Court in The Hague.

Netherlands – Art Appreciation

Lilith's other dress resembles Vincent van Gogh's *Irises* painting.

She will be attending an event at the Van Gogh Museum in Amsterdam, both to enjoy viewing his paintings and to help recover lost art looted during World War II.

She is a Monuments Woman, working with museum curators to finish the work of repatriating whatever remains missing.

The United Nations Office of Outer Space Affairs

Lilith will be making another stop on her trip to Europe – to Vienna, Austria.

Ileandra has been traveling along be with her.

This part of the trip will be of particular interest to the alien, because this is where the international treaties on human activities in outer space are housed.

There are treaties about the peaceful use of outer space, the sharing of the Moon, and the regulation of orbital debris and the damage it causes, both in space and when it falls back to Earth. (Sometimes, it doesn't burn up in the atmosphere on the way down.)

There is a treaty for astronauts that guarantees that they may rescue each other in space, despite of any disagreements that their governments may be having back on the planet's surface. Space is a dangerous environment, and humans cannot afford to let political or other difference endanger themselves or others.

Memorial Day at Arlington National Cemetery

Antoinette will play the music from the movies *Saving Private* Ryan and *The Monuments Men*.

She will do this outside the Women in Military Service for America Memorial, which is located at the entrance to Arlington National Cemetery, just across the Potomac River from the Lincoln Memorial.

This structure is called a hemicycle because of its half-circle shape.

Inside the Military Women's Memorial (another name used for it) is a database with computer terminals. Anyone with a relative who served in the U.S. military can look her up on it.

Antoinette looked up her great-aunt, who served as a WASP during World War II. That acronym stands for Women Air Service Pilots; they delivered newly manufactured fighter planes to the war theaters in Europe and Asia.

June

Gay Pride Parade

Father's Day

Juneteenth

Walt Disney Concert Hall

Elizabeth Park Rose Garden

Summer Solstice Celebration

RESTORATION HARDWARE
ORIGINS
THE NEW YORK CITY COUNCIL

Gay Pride Parade in New York City

Lilith will be attending, with New York politicians, the annual Gay Pride Parade in New York City. They will be walking in that parade to support their constituents and enjoy the day.

Each year in early June, the city holds this beautiful, fun parade. Thousands of spectators come out to watch and enjoy the music as floats with dancing drag queens go by.

The music that blares from the floats is mostly 1980s pop songs, such as Boy George and the Culture Club's "Karma Chameleon" and Frankie Goes to Hollywood's "Relax".

Everyone has a good time out in the sun at this event.

Father's Day

Antoinette's father loves strawberries. This is ideal for a dessert to honor her dad, because they are in season. She will bake one of his favorite desserts, something that she created: Strawberry Key Lime Curd Tart. She will go to a local farm to get fresh, ripe, juicy, perfect strawberries for it.

Then she will play the fifth movement of Gustav Mahler's Symphony No. 3 for him – it's one of his favorite pieces of music. It is called *Lustig im Tempo und keck im Ausdruck* (Cheerful in tempo and cheeky in expression), and is played in F major.

Juneteenth

On June 19, 1865, at the end of the U.S. Civil War, General Gordon Granger was in Texas, where he ordered the final enforcement of President Abraham Lincoln's Emancipation Proclamation. With that, slavery was finally over with in the entire United States of America, and everyone knew it.

Juneteenth is the holiday that celebrates this.

Lilith attended a celebration of Juneteenth in Washington, D.C. People painted murals to beautify the sides of old, tall, brick apartment buildings and decorated a newly paved street with huge letters. The letters spell out "JUNETEENTH" and feature bright colors and images.

People were enjoying themselves until the fun was interrupted by a racist lunatic with an assault rifle. He sprayed bullets at the gathering, wounding a grandmother in the upper arm, and a teenage boy in the leg.

Lilith saw him before he could fire more than a few shots. She took out her wand and stunned him. With another flick of her wand, she disassembled his weapon, and then had the pieces and the bullets in ziplock bags for the police. She put her wand away before anyone saw it.

Once the injured people were attended to, the festivities resumed, because everyone was determined not to let a monster with a gun control their lives and their plans.

But Lilith is frustrated with the lack of gun laws in the United States. The 2nd Amendment of the U.S. Constitution is deliberately misread by gun lobbyists, ignoring the part about a "well-regulated militia" and the purpose of that amendment: to have armed forces, not a gun in every hand that wants one.

A potluck party will be held in the late afternoon. Lilith made chocolate chip almond oatmeal cookies to share at the event.

Disney Music Concert

Antoinette is ready to perform at the Walt Disney Concert Hall in Los Angeles.

She will be playing the music of *Fantasia* in the first part of the concert.

After the intermission, she will play themes from *Aladdin*, *Beauty and the Beast*, *Pocahontas*, *Maleficent*, and *The Fox and the Hound*.

Antoinette has found a gourmet bakery in the area, so she brought cardamom cupcakes with rosewater frosting to share with the orchestra during the intermission.

Elizabeth Park Rose Garden

Straddling the border between Hartford and West Hartford in Connecticut is the famous rose garden of Elizabeth Park. The park is named for Elizabeth Pond, the wife of the founder.

Antoinette will be playing there, in the gazebo at the center of the rose garden. It is an amazing structure made of twisted branches topped with turf and surrounded by climbing roses.

Her concert will take place during the early evening, and will feature Claude Debussy's *Claire de Lune*. A pianist will accompany her.

A Feast for Her Senses!

Ileandra is having a wonderful time following Antoinette around.

She is doing okay being out during the daytime, thanks to a pair of sunglasses and a hat, and there is always a place in the shade if things get too bright. It's all worth it.

The roses smell wonderful, and each one is a unique variety.

The alien is enjoying the wide repertoire of music that her friend plays, too. She has heard some of this music on her ship, en route to Earth, but hearing it played live is even better.

Antoinette has left the alien to her own devices, free to wander around the entire rose garden, and see every blossom. She knows that the botanist must be very happy right now.

Ileandra even saw a honey bee working on a pastel pink rose.

The bee turned and looked back at her as if to say, "What do YOU want?!" It was simultaneously amazing and amusing.

Summer Solstice Coven

For June 21st, the longest day of the year, Lilith is hosting an outdoor, evening, summer solstice party.

She has invited her best friend, Antoinette, who is attending without her violin, and their visitor from outer space, Ileandra, to enjoy it with her.

The summer solstice occurs at the loveliest time of year, when the most beautiful flowers are in bloom and berry season is just getting underway.

Because of this, Antoinette has brought a raspberry tart that she made, and Lilith will serve iced fruit tea. Ileandra is looking forward to trying the tea and experiencing a human celebration of the growing season.

July

Independence Day

Witch Trials Memorial

Butterfly Habitat Event

Evening at Highclere Castle – Downton Abbey Theme

Happy 4ᵗʰ of July!

Antoinette has been chosen to sing our national anthem, "The Star-Spangled Banner" by attorney Francis Scott Key, at the annual birthday party for the United States, which is held on the lawns of the National Mall between the U.S. Capitol and the Lincoln Memorial.

She will stand by the Lincoln Memorial and sing at the end of the event, just before the spectacular pyrotechnics show of red, white, and blue fireworks that closes the event.

When it is over, she and Lilith will meet their boyfriends and share a raspberry-blueberry tart together. Antoinette made it.

Witch Trials – A Herstorical Memorial for Independent Women

Lilith Hermione Wandcraft has an outfit to wear to an event commemorating women who were hanged as witches in the 17th century in America.

Women were murdered in Windsor, Connecticut, Salem, Massachusetts, and many other places. They were not actually witches. They neither knew nor used magic. They were simply independent personalities, and that angered the people around them. It was a bad time, one in which anyone who was different was not safe.

The outfit is a jacket with a cotton print over a solid skirt. This was an 18th century outfit, featuring a contrasting pattern over a solid fabric, but it was what she wanted to wear.

When she is done with this event, she can wear it at another event at Monticello, Thomas Jefferson's home in Virginia. The nation's 3rd president had an extensive garden, and she will be sharing her knowledge of the plants that he grew.

She might as well get more use from this outfit.

Butterfly Habitat Event

Antoinette is helping Lilith to promote an initiative to expand and protect existing Monarch butterfly habitats. The goal to induce states and the federal government to plant milkweed along highways.

Monarch butterflies migrate northwest from Mexico to Canada and back again, stopping at four points along this route. By the time they reach the next point, they are members of the next generation. There is no persuading them to choose any other stopping points.

Monarch butterflies get their name from the Dutch royal House of Orange due to their color.

The event will be held at the National Butterfly Center on the Texas-Mexico border, which is threatened by plans for a border wall. The reason for this choice of venue for the event is to call attention to the plight of the butterfly habitat; the wall would put 70 percent of the habitat behind that wall, in Mexico, dividing it and damaging it during and after construction.

Antoinette will sing Claude Debussy's *Les Papillons*, which is a song composed from Théophile Gautier's poem about butterflies. (Her dress, by the way, has butterfly sleeves.)

Butterfly Effect

Lilith is determined that a small change in policy — to preserve the butterfly habitat — will result in a larger result. The hope is that there will be a greater appreciation for preserving the ecosystem than for sealing off the border between Mexico and the United States.

Walls are pointless.

They can be dug under, flown over, and sailed around.

They can even be climbed over.

No one benefits from walls other than the people who supply the construction materials for and the labor to build them.

After that, humans die in the desert trying to cross the wall, while some manage to get under, over, and around it.

Meanwhile, the butterfly population, an essential pollinator species, dies because it loses a crucial, irreplaceable point along its migration route.

None of that makes sense.

Lilith has brought several senators and representatives to attend Antoinette's event, plus some attorneys from the Environmental Protection Agency, all of whom will be drafting legislation to address this issue.

Her dress has butterfly sleeves, too.

Almost as Hot as at Home

Texas in July on Earth is really, really hot. Ileandra has been reading some of the books in the personal libraries of her hosts, including some by climate change journalists.

Antoinette has one by an author who lives in this state, so the alien studied for this trip by reading it. Still, nothing prepared her for the shock of daytime heat. It's like nighttime on her planet, but with bright sunlight added.

That means that her planet is hotter than Texas in July during the day. Lilith gave her a pair of sunglasses, and Antoinette gave her a hat.

It's still tough for her.

There was a tour of the butterfly sanctuary, which meant spending a significant amount of time outside in the intense heat and bright light.

She saw about half of it, and then had to go inside to take an air-conditioning break. That break lasted twenty minutes. By the time she was able to go back outside, people were coming back inside.

At least they enjoyed Antoinette's violin concert, heard Lilith announce the speakers, and listened to them inside the visitor center.

Ileandra thought she was failing to appreciate the visit until Lilith and Antoinette told her, as they drove away together, that it was difficult for them to spend a long time out in this heat, too.

If that's true, how will humans cope with a rapidly warming ecosystem?

Evening at Highclere Castle

Antoinette has been commissioned to perform at Highclere Castle in Hampshire, England at a promotional event for a *Downton Abbey* production, playing the theme from that television show.

This 1910s gown was made for that occasion. Antoinette's curls almost, but not quite, cover up the button, which depicts a woman with a flower in her hair in the Art Nouveau style.

Tea and scones will be served, and a museum walk-through will be held by the real-life countess.

A museum walk-through means that each room will be roped off, making a path for visitors to walk through and view it without going randomly everywhere, and no touching will be allowed. This is standard museum protocol.

A historian will be in each room to talk about the décor, the art, and the family history that took place – and still does – in there.

This was done once on the television show, so fans will know what to expect when they visit Highclere Castle in real life.

Culture Shock

It was one thing for Ileandra to know, in theory, that her ancestors had a similar class system in her people's distant past. It was quite another to see a historic house museum…well, historic castle, really…with that lifestyle on display.

And to think that it still has an earl and countess living in it!

These aristocrats can no longer afford the lavish lifestyle that this place once offered, but the vestiges of it were apparent with the butler who settled her and Antoinette into place for the evening.

It is a showcase of unequal resource distribution, one that she has traveled far across the Milky Way galaxy to see.

It was surreal to the little alien – and quite an adventure.

She enjoyed keeping her human friend company and seeing it all.

August

Earth Overshoot Day

State Dinner with the President and First Lady of France

Smithsonian Museum Hall of First Ladies

Visit to Provence, France – Concerts in Grasse and
Cannes

Tanglewood on Parade

Organic and Small Farming v. GMOs and Agribusiness

Berry Festival

Earth Overshoot Day

Every year since 1969, there has been an Earth Overshoot Day.

Earth Overshoot Day measures the point at which the planet as a whole – meaning the humans living on it – has used up a year's worth of resources.

Before 1969, we didn't need to measure this, because our resource use went all the way to December 31st. Then this point started to move backwards through the year. We are now operating at a deficit, as if we have 5 Earths.

Each nation also has its own Earth Overshoot Day. The wealthier the nation, the sooner in the year its overshoot point. The United States already had its overshoot day on March 14th.

This year, the planet's overshoot day will be on August 1st.

During the coronavirus pandemic, it was later in the month because so many people weren't driving much, but we're back to our usual lifestyle now, so the depletion of resources has picked up momentum…again.

Lilith is giving an interview on CBS's *60 Minutes* about the damage humans are inflicting on the Earth and the reasons why little is being done about it. She will talk about the policies to mitigate this by the current presidential administration, and the policies that it is working to repair, which were largely undone by the previous one. This is an ongoing impediment to any serious progress in saving the planet.

The main driver of all this is sheet numbers of humans in the form of overpopulation. There are currently over 8 billion humans. Our planet can only support less than 2 billion. We also need a degrowth economy.

Antoinette will be shown in the segment, playing music from the movie score of *Inferno*, the overpopulation movie based on Dan Brown's novel of the same name.

The Alien Botanist Approves

Ileandra is impressed that humans are tracking the depletion of their planet. She hadn't expected that.

Despite this effort, however, she realizes that few of them even notice it.

They are busy with their daily lives and routines, and with acquiring enough resources to continue them. Most humans don't have time to stop and learn about Earth Overshoot Day or other ecological problems.

This affects their decisions, including voting.

It is frustrating to watch another planet go down the same path as hers did, knowing that, if enough humans actually survive – with educated humans valued and respected – someday, on Earth, there will be botanists just like her, trying to save the few plants that are left. Perhaps humans will have to travel to faraway planets to collect more food-bearing plants, like she does.

Her planet is slightly larger than Earth. It had 14 billion people on it when its resources were critically depleted…until many died off, due to insufficient food supplies. Her planet couldn't support that many people, so it simply didn't.

Ileandra's planet now has 750 million people on it.

That would be about right if her people can remediate its ecosystem, but it is too hot, and they now must grow food in greenhouses and go outside only at night.

That is why her eyes are so huge. She has good night vision, too.

Earth would fare far better with half a billion people – 500 million.

The problem is getting to that point without depriving any existing humans of their lives.

Too many want to reproduce, regardless of overshoot!

White House State Dinner – France's Leaders Visit

The President and First Lady of France have come to visit, and a state dinner is being put on at the White House.

Antoinette and Lilith each have beautiful berry-patterned gowns for this event. The idea behind this is to be wearing the red, white, and blue colors of both the United States and France.

Antoinette will be providing the entertainment by playing her violin for the partygoers once dinner is over. She will play music from *Star Trek Beyond* by Michael Giacchino.

In honor of the French visitors, lavender desserts will be served: lavender crème brulée and honey lavender ice cream.

Lilith has a lot to do.

Her agenda involves the United Nations treaty of 1971, called the Convention on International Liability for Space Objects. These objects include anything made by humans and launched into Earth's orbit, because that area is part of the ecosystem. Functioning as well as defunct satellites, plus small objects lost while astronauts are at work, are covered by this agreement.

Lilith must work the room, meeting with anyone she can talk to about protecting the ecosystem of the Earth and its 5 layers of atmosphere. Her focus is on the mesosphere and the thermosphere.

Just above the Karman line, thousands of satellites are in orbit in the thermosphere. Higher up in the thermosphere, the International Space Station and the Webb Telescope (and other telescopes) orbit. The Earth and its space environment must be kept peaceful and free of debris if they are to be safe places to live and work.

Lilith's goals are to convince the politicians to fund a space vacuum cleaner to collect loose debris, and to write and promulgate a treaty banning the detonation of defunct satellites in space, because that causes debris fields that move as fast as bullets fired from a gun.

Dinner Conversation with an Alien

Lilith will quietly introduce Ileandra to the Presidents of the United States and France, telling them that she is an alien botanist, visiting to observe human culture while collecting plant samples.

After that, she will leave the alien at the table with them during dessert, and let them chat.

Ileandra will take this opportunity to share what she has observed thus far, and explain the ecological and political history of her own planet. She will warn them of the destructive path that humanity is on, comparing the Earth to her own home.

It may not change the course of Earth's ecological use and abuse by humans, but she can't visit without trying to help.

Ileandra has a beautiful iris dress for the occasion. It has a gray background. As she sewed it, Antoinette's couturière quipped that this would give the alien not only a Small Gray environmental suit, but also a gray gown.

The alien and her friend were amused.

In a way, both outfits are work clothes – for different sorts of work.

First Ladies Event

Antoinette has a gown in lavender and a pattern called "Cecile Embroidered Suffragette." (British women who fought for the right to vote were called "suffragettes"; the artist of this fabric pattern is British.)

She will be playing just outside the exhibit of first ladies' gowns at the Smithsonian's National Museum of American History.

First Lady Dr. Jill Biden will be there, and so will former First Ladies Hillary Rodham Clinton, Laura Bush, and Michelle Obama.

Antoinette will be playing music from the woman suffrage movie *Iron Jawed Angels* and from the Ruth Bader Ginsburg biopic *On the Basis of Sex.*

Visit to Provence, France – Concerts in Grasse and Cannes

Antoinette is following up her appearance at the White House by traveling to the South of France, to the region of Provence.

Her friends are coming with her; Lilith is taking a working vacation to bring some secure documents to someone at a bistro, and Ileandra wouldn't miss this trip. Antoinette and Lilith are ladies in lavender for the Cannes concert.

Provence is where the Cannes Film Festival is held each May.

Antoinette will play in the Théâtre de Grasse and at the Palais des Festivals et des Congrès in Cannes (which is where the Cannes Film Festival is held each May, by invitation only).

She will play music by Claude Debussy, Wolfgang Amadeus Mozart, and John Williams.

Her couturière has outfitted all three women for the trip.

Vacances – A Rare Treat!

"Vacances" means vacation in French.

Lilith has just one thing to do, and then she is free to enjoy this trip.

It is a rare treat for her, and she is enjoying it thoroughly.

France has some of the most delicious food to enjoy, and as it is late August, the South of France is full of people enjoying the summer weather.

Lilith has been walking along the promenades by the beaches, visiting French bookshops, and going into chocolateries.

This is great fun!

PARFUMEUR
Fragonard
PARFUMEUR

Grasse – Concert and Parfumerie Excursion

Antoinette will play music from the movie score from *A Good Year*, which is about, among other things, a winery and people in Provence, France.

But this is also a vacation for her; she will have some fun, too.

The best perfumes in the world are made at a place in Grasse. Antoinette will take her friends on a tour of the Fragonard parfumerie, and to surprise Lilith and give Ileandra a special treat, she will buy them perfumes in the shop. For herself, she would like a lavender-jasmine-rose scent.

She is glad to be showing an alien botanist all this.

She knows that the Earth must be careful to protect it, and she loves it.

Earthly Delights in France

Ileandra is beside herself on this trip with wonder, delight, and wistfulness. Is this what her planet once had to offer its people — delectable tastes, sweet scents, and beautiful sights?!

It is all lost now, lost to time and a failure to have appreciated and protected it.

She is glad to be among humans who do appreciate what their planet has, and who try to protect it.

When it is gone and there is only money from it, that money won't last.

And then it will all just be gone.

She knows.

Her planet is proof.

Concert at Seiji Ozawa Hall, Tanglewood

Antoinette will be performing in the Seiji Ozawa Hall at "Tanglewood on Parade" in Lenox, Massachusetts, in the Berkshire Hills area. This venue is named for the famous Japanese conductor who performed each piece as the composer intended, rather than editorializing any. Antoinette loves that!

Among the pieces she will play are the works of John Williams, the movie score composer and former director of the Boston Pops. Her favorites include *Born on the Fourth of July*, *Indiana Jones*, *E.T.: The Extra-Terrestrial*, *Star Wars*, *Empire of the Sun*, and his compositions for the *Harry Potter* movies.

A meal will be served for the patron donors and the musicians under a tent on the lawns of Tanglewood. The weather forecast is for a very hot day, so she will appreciate the dessert of berry sorbet.

Organic and Small Farming

Lilith Hermione will be visiting organic farmers and other small, independent farmers in what are often thought of as "flyover states".

She intends to get their individual stories and then return to Washington, D.C. to share them with the president.

The idea is to develop strategies to protect the business interests of these farmers against those of big agribusinesses, which have become so big that they are antitrust violations, and use insecticides and GMO seeds that drift, carried by the wind, over to other properties, damaging their crops. This interferes with organic farmers' ability to maintain their status as organic farmers.

She and the president will draft regulations against this for the Environmental Protection Agency to enforce.

Berry Festival

Ileandra is about to have a feast of Earthly delights.

She will take home cuttings of raspberry, blackberry, blueberry, and strawberry plants. (Well, she already had plenty of strawberry samples!) She is enjoying each taste on her visit.

As for Antoinette and Lilith, they love berries, and look forward to berry season each year. They both love to make delicious desserts with berries, and can't get enough of them. They eat bowlfuls of berries as often as they can. The idea of a berry farmers' market and festival is too enticing to miss.

It is held in a garden with a lovely lathhouse, which they usually take photographs under. Ileandra is in it this time.

When the event is over, they will take their alien guest back to Lilith's place and make a cold treat that they all love: smoothies!

September

Labor Day

Night at the Wadsworth Atheneum

Agricultural Fair Season

Mushroom Festival

Purple Rain Concert

Labor Day Picnic

The warm season is ending, and Antoinette will be sending it off with an outdoor concert. It will be held in the Sunken Gardens of the Hillstead Museum in Farmington, Connecticut, during a picnic. The museum will also be open for walk-through tours.

Fried chicken, biscuits, fresh greens and avocado salad, and chocolate chip cookies will be served.

Antoinette will play music from Marvel Comics movies: *X-Men*, *Iron Man*, *Captain America*, and *The Avengers*. Why not? Everyone is out for an evening of fun.

Night at the Wadsworth Atheneum

A gala ball for donors and docents (volunteer guides) will be held at the nation's oldest atheneum in Hartford, Connecticut.

Antoinette will play concertos as part of the evening's entertainment.

Her gown depicts the theme of the evening: floral art. Not only will paintings with flowers be on display – including the famous flower paintings by Georgia O'Keeffe – but a garden club's competition of floral arrangements will be shown in each gallery.

The event will be catered by the finest restaurants in the city, including the creations of dessert chefs: pumpkin pecan cheesecake and white chocolate cheesecake with raspberry sauce.

Agricultural Fair Season

Lilith has a lot of events to attend in October, most of them state fairs. It will be a lot of fun, because she will be meeting farmers and craftspeople from all over the United States, and tasting the foods that they produce.

Each state is known for different recipes, based on the crops that are grown in them. Lilith will get to enjoy apple cider, cheddar cheese, lobster rolls, peach pie, crab cakes, cornbread, and many other treats during her travels.

The political purpose behind her trip is to promote the rights of small farmers and organic farmers. Insecticide use and big agribusiness threaten the livelihoods of these farmers by attacking the biodiversity and business model that they depend on.

Keeping the ecosystem healthy and family farms economically viable is crucial to the continued availabilty of the wonderful foods that she will experience as she visits each state.

Sometimes, a politician's job includes great fun! Apple Raisin Pie with a Maple Leaf Crust is just one dessert that she looks forward to eating.

Apple Cider Season

Antoinette is with Lilith at the Big E – the Eastern States Exposition, which is held annually in West Springfield, Massachusetts. Their boyfriends are with them, too, and the four of them are having a lovely day off together.

The fair includes farm animals – sheep, cows, horses, chickens, and even honey bees – plus crafts and rides. There is a late 18th-century village called Storrowton, complete with historic interpreters in period clothing. At the far end of the fair ground is a row of exhibit halls for each of the New England states: Massachusetts, Connecticut, Rhode Island, New Hampshire, Vermont, and Maine.

In these halls, Antoinette and Lilith will eat their dinner by going from stall to stall. They will have blueberry muffins and lobster rolls in the Maine building, apple cider doughnuts, apple cider, and apple pie with cheddar cheese in the Vermont building, honey in the Connecticut building, and so on.

They will also tour Storrowton Village to see a blacksmith at work and a teacher explaining how education worked in rural towns two centuries ago (children brought whatever books their families owned, and the teachers taught them out of those).

CONNECTICUT

Stares – They Go Both Ways

Ileandra is with Antoinette, Lilith, and their boyfriends at the Big E.

Earth is starting to get a bit chilly for her, but Antoinette's couturière has thought of that, and she has a warm jacket to wear.

People keep staring at her as they wait in lines and walk by.

She seems to stare back with her huge eyes, but she's really just looking around at everything.

Some of the staring is awkward, but sometimes it amuses her, and she turns to the staring humans with a little smile. That stops it…for a little while, until they move on and new people catch sight of her.

But the alien doesn't care. The people only stare, and pretty much mind their own business. It's not like they can be sure that she's an alien, and it's rude to bother strangers.

Ileandra is having fun wandering around the fairgrounds with her human friends. The boyfriends know who and what she is, and have taken it in stride, though they did ask if she has a boyfriend.

She smiled and said that she does; he's an entomologist. He studies insects. She took some brochures from the beehive displays to show him when she goes back to her ship.

Mushroom Festival

Lilith will be going with the secretary of agriculture for the United States to visit mushroom farms and attend the Kennett Mushroom Festival in Kennett Square, Pennsylvania.

Pennsylvania leads the nation in growing mushrooms. This started with the Quakers in the 19th century, because they grew carnations, and wanted to do something useful with the wasted space underneath. Mushrooms require no light to grow, and are made up of 90 percent water, so this crop was just right for their farms.

Mushrooms are best planted in the spring, and harvested until late fall.

$5.99
FRESH MUSHROOM
19.50
DRIED PORCINI
MUSHROOM
$24.50
LB
DRIED WOOD
EAR MUSHROOM
$22.99
LB
DRIED BLACK
TRUMPET
MUSHROOM
$19.99
LB

Purple Rain Concert

Antoinette will be participating in an event to honor the late – and great – rock star, Prince Rogers Nelson. It will be held at his Paisley Park estate, now the Paisley Park Museum, in Chanhassen, Minnesota.

His unique electric cloud guitar will be on loan from the Smithsonian Museum, to be played along with the violin, drums, synthesizer, and other instruments.

Songs from the movie *Purple Rain* will be featured, including "When Doves Cry," "Baby I'm a Star," and, of course, the eponymous "Purple Rain".

Her dress is made from cotton fabric that is comfortable to wear, and that evokes the theme of the event.

The performers will have some Pumpkin Spice Cupcakes with Purple White Chocolate Cream Cheese Frosting at the party later on.

October

Going Away Party

Antoinette and Lilith will miss Ileandra, but it is getting too cold for her here. She has collected lots of plants, and it's time for her to go home.

So, rather than focus on missing her, they are having a party for her, so that they can say good-bye to her, and that they hope she will visit them again.

At this party, the alien's human friends have shown her yet another wonderful fruit: pomegranates. These fruits are full of seeds that make delicious red juice. Pomegranates are native to Iran. They are also produced in India, China, Turkey, Spain, Pakistan, Syria, Iraq, and the United States.

Ileandra was relieved to hear that; she doesn't really want to deal with snakes in India again (she has had some scary experiences that she prefers not to repeat!), and she knows that in Iran, she cannot dress comfortably while she works, as she must wear a long, cumbersome black robe in case she is seen from a distance.

This will give her another excuse to see her friends – she can go with them to California sometime and get a pomegranate plant.

Meanwhile, Antoinette bought a pomegranate at the local grocery store for the alien to take home with her. It will tide her over in her laboratory until she can get that plant.

Antoinette and Lilith felt much better about the end of the visit when she said that. She'll be back!

Parting Thoughts

Ileandra is going home.

She has collected lots of plant cuttings on her visit, and observed human culture as she worked.

She enjoyed her visit, meeting humans, and watching them simultaneously appreciate and ruin their habitat.

It has been a bittersweet trip for her to see this, because she is about to go home and work to make the plants she has collected thrive in her own planet's ecosystem – an ecosystem that her ancestors ruined the same way that she is now seeing humans ruin theirs.

She hopes that we will come to our senses in time, but is not optimistic.

She has thanked Antoinette and Lilith for their hospitality, their great help in collecting so many fruit-bearing and flowering plants, and told them what is on her mind.

They thanked her for telling them all that, and they will miss her.

They're on Their Own Again

Lilith came to Avon, Connecticut with Antoinette and Ileandra to see the alien leave and say good-bye.

It was just a back yard for a departure point, but it was quiet, no one else was around, and that was how they preferred it.

They made her one last strawberry purée drink, and she was off.

Her ship briefly appeared, hovering over the back yard late at night.

There was a flash of light, and another alien, a male with short hair, was standing at the far end of the lawn, just in front of the honeysuckle bush. He waved to Ileandra.

Ileandra walked over to him, and they smiled at each other.

They both looked back at Antoinette and Lilith, who were standing just outside the kitchen door in the dimly lit back yard. Antoinette's cat was sitting up in his basket, staring out the window at the parting alien He knew she was leaving.

Antoinette and Lilith waved. The aliens waved back, and with another flash of light, they were gone, and then so was their ship.

Indigenous Peoples Day

The Indigenous Peoples of North America don't need any help to celebrate their own culture. They can do that better than any other people can. That is usually how it works with any culture.

This day is about keeping the native tribes at the forefront of the thoughts of policy makers in government, and in the minds of citizens. With that practice maintained – and not just on a holiday devoted to this purpose – the hope is to keep sacred lands protected by safeguarding the ecosystem from profit-driven corporations and other human construction projects.

To this end, a concert will be held in the John F. Kennedy Center for the Performing Arts in Washington, D.C. The National Symphony Orchestra will have Antoinette appear as its solo violinist. The performance will be broadcast on PBS and NPR.

The program will include selections from the movie scores of *Dances with Wolves* (composed by John Barry), *Windtalkers* (composed by James Horner), and *The Last of the Mohicans* (composed by Trevor Jones and Randy Edelman).

The scene will shift back and forth between Antoinette and the orchestra and overhead views of each of the 63 national parks and 133 national monuments, in the United States, with text naming each one as they are shown.

The proceeds from this concert will be spent on park preservation.

Antoinette is looking forward to visiting with her best friend Lilith, and will stay with her at her Georgetown house. Their boyfriends will be there, too.

Protecting National Parks and Monuments

Lilith is attending the Indigenous Peoples Concert to highlight her next project: she has visits planned with leaders of various Native American tribes.

She will be traveling with the Secretary of the Interior to meet them.

The purpose is to protect U.S. national parks and monuments and lands that are sacred to the tribes from mining, oil and shale production, and other commercial activities that would destroy them.

Boundaries of national parks and monuments that have been shrunk are to be restored.

The native people have a saying: "You can't eat money."

They are absolutely right. Once a natural resource is destroyed to get something as ephemeral as money, the next generation will have nothing.

Here is the Cree proverb about it in its entirety:

> *Only when the last tree has died,*
> *The last river has been poisoned,*
> *The last fish has been caught,*
> *Will we realize that you can't eat money.*

Cat Love – Ailurophilia!

Antoinette will be performing some songs from the Andrew Lloyd Weber musical *Cats* to raise money for cat shelters across the nation. This means that she will be stopping at various cat cafés to visit the cats, share coffee with patrons, and play her violin and sing.

Lilith will be traveling with her to drum up some political publicity for the enactment of laws in every state recognizing the right of animals to a happy, healthy, and safe life.

As usual, their couturière has outfitted them for the tour, in a theme relevant to it.

Meanwhile, back at home, Antoinette has a wonderful cat: Specter the Spectator. He likes to be her at-home audience as she plays the violin and sings. He also smiles a lot, as shown in this image.

Happy Hallowe'en!

Antoinette will be playing the movie scores of *Beetlejuice* and *The Nightmare Before Christmas* at the Walt Disney Concert Hall in Los Angeles.

Lilith will be in the area to meet with California politicians about 2 plans: one is to make the nation's largest economy go green, particularly with electric vehicles, and the other is aimed at mitigating and remediating wildlife loss with a plan to build underpasses and overpasses on roads and highways for animals to safely cross them.

They will meet after the concert and get some Hallowe'en desserts and coffee, and have a nice, relaxed visit and chat.

A Witch in Her Traditional Attire

Part of the fun of Hallowe'en is sartorial. Lilith has everything she needs to dress up as what she is: a witch. Her attire evokes traditional Wiccan customs and ancient culture.

Why do we think of witches in black? Often, they lived alone, widows in mourning for their husbands. Notice that Lilith wears lots of colors; she is not a widow. She has a boyfriend!

What about the herbs that witches worked with? Witches were medicine women. They knew the plants of their local ecosystem, the medicinal properties of those plants, and how to brew tinctures, balms, and potions from them. Anyone with an ailment would visit their local witch.

Then the Burning Times came, leaving one woman alive in every village in Europe. This was around 1482, when the Catholic pope decided to stamp out any competing religions, particularly the nature-worshipping Wicca, which focused on revering a goddess and respecting independence in women. Hallowe'en, called Samhain by Wiccans, honors the dead. It is not scary, despite the horror movies marketed during its season.

Notice that one of the items in Lilith's bag is a bundle of sage with a Ruth Bader Ginsburg image wrapped around it. There is something on the opposite side, with pins in it…something that shall not be described here. Perhaps you can guess what it depicts. Happy Hallowe'en!

November

Election Day

Veterans' Day

Pardoned Turkeys

Thanksgiving

Election Day

The first Tuesday in November is Election Day in the United States.

It's time to vote for President of the United States again.

The nation is as divided ideologically as it was when the Civil War broke out in the mid-19th century.

This time, however, it's about other things: keeping things moving forward to maintain a democratic, civil society that doesn't seek to control people versus turning the clock back to the 1950s.

Shall we have reproductive control by individual women, including abortion, birth control, and any medical procedure that preserves a woman's health and autonomy as soon as she needs it?

Shall women be free to have educations and careers?

Shall LGBTQA+ people be allowed to feel safe being themselves?

Shall we maintain a legal firewall between religions and government?

Shall fascism be treated as treason and criminal intent?

Shall voting continue to be possible for all, complete with absentee voting via the U.S. Postal Service (Antoinette does that)?

We hope so.

Vote like democracy depends on it, because it does.

Antoinette is dressed for Election Day.

She will be playing on the steps of the Lincoln Memorial.

Come and hear her play themes from *The Post* (a movie about freedom of the press), *Harriet* (a biographical movie about Harriet Tubman), *Selma* (a civil rights march movie), and she shall conclude with "Enter Lord Vader" from *Star Wars: Episode III – The Revenge of the Sith* and "The Return of the Jedi" from *Star Wars: Episode VI – Ewok Celebration*.

Veterans Day

Lilith is busy.

She is at the Walter Reed National Medical Military Center, visiting patients. Starting with this hospital, Lilith will be making sure that Veterans hospitals around the nation are staffed and equipped with everything that they need, and that mental health services and job opportunities are available.

This process won't be complete without asking the patients themselves what they need, and what they wish would be done differently.

Returning soldiers often have PTSD (post-traumatic stress disorder). For their service of exposing themselves to horrific situations in war zones around the world, they deserve to come home to reliable support systems.

Pardoned Turkeys

The president pardons 2 turkeys each year before Thanksgiving.

The turkeys stay at the Williard InterContinental Washington Hotel, which happens to be the same one that Antoinette is staying at.

Antoinette will stay in the Jenny Lind Suite, named for a famous 19th-century Swedish opera singer. She will enjoy a bath in an enormous tub with a huge window over it that looks out at the Washington Monument.

Her boyfriend will join her at the hotel so that he can hear her sing and play on her visit to Washington, D.C. He lives in Manhattan, and works as an astronomy professor at Columbia University.

Antoinette and her boyfriend will eat at the Café du Parc, which is the hotel's restaurant. The turkeys are fed in their room.

She will not visit them, but she will see them on the White House lawn, where she will meet Lilith and watch the hilarious pardoning take place.

They are looking forward to finding out what names this year's turkeys are given. Past pairs of names have included: Cobbler and Gobbler, Popcorn and Caramel, Drumstick and Wishbone, and Chocolate and Chip.

Antoinette will play music from the movie *Addams Family Values* – and feature the tunes from the scenes at Wednesday and Pugsley's camp, during the Thanksgiving play fiasco.

Lilith has told her that the president said he is "looking forward to hearing that!" when she told him what her friend will be playing!

Thanksgiving

Lilith's boyfriend has surprised her with not just a visit for the holiday, but dinner at a renowned gourmet farm-to-table restaurant.

He is taking time off from his work as a degrowth economics consultant at the Brookings Institution.

He knew that the president wouldn't need his girlfriend on this particular day, so he took advantage of the opportunity to be alone with her and to spoil her. She enjoys good food, and appreciates the sources it comes from and the work and artistry put into it.

Well…he knows that. She has given him plenty of wonderful meals.

They will enjoy their meal, and then go for a walk along the National Mall to look at the monuments.

December

Concert with the Philadelphia Orchestra

Resting for the Holiday Concert

Holiday Concert

Happy Winter Solstice!

New Year's Eve – Happy New Year!

Concert with the Philadelphia Orchestra

Antoinette will play with the Philadelphia Orchestra in early December.

The program will include selections from the music of composer Aaron Copeland:

Lincoln Portrait, narrated by actor Matt Damon, will be first.

It will be followed by *Billy the Kid* and *Rodeo*.

After the intermission, they will play *Fanfare for the Common Man*, and conclude with *Quiet City*.

Resting for the Holiday Concert

Antoinette is lounging in her bathrobe before the holiday concert.

She has made her favorite holiday cookies to enjoy with her boyfriend: Viennese Crescents, which are little walnut-butter crescent moons dusted with vanilla bean sugar, and pressed butter cookies with a tree shape that have been sprinkled with alternating red and green sugar.

Happy Winter Solstice!

Antoinette will be playing at the Bushnell Center for the Performing Arts with the Hartford Symphony Orchestra. She will perform classic Christmas music and the movie score of *The Grinch* by Danny Elfman on her violin, and then sing *Candles in the Window* by John Williams.

The city's finest dessert chefs will be catering the orchestra's after-party. Antoinette is looking forward to trying Chocolate-Glazed Poached Anjou Pears with Apricots and Raisins.

A Wiccan Treat

Lilith is having a Winter Solstice celebration of her own as she spends it with her boyfriend and family. She has made their favorite cake: Chocolate Orange Cake with Grated Chocolate.

Everyone is happy to be together and catch up on news.

Happy New Year!

Antoinette is resplendent in her "Musical Gown in Black and Gold".

She is ready to perform at the Metropolitan Opera in New York City. She will sing an aria from Wolfgang Amadeus Mozart's *The Magic Flute*. After the intermission, she will play Georg Friederich Händel's *Music for the Royal Fireworks* with the orchestra on her violin.

She will end the evening in the perfect way: with a slice of chocolate hazelnut cake. She has made it, and packed it to bring to the concert hall to share with her colleagues.

Her boyfriend will join them backstage to have some of that cake, and then they will go home to their apartment in Chelsea.

Antoinette wishes everyone a Happy New Year, and hopes that your wishes come true and your resolutions pay off!

Background on the Dolls

My mother, who can always be counted upon to stop at a tag sale, noticed Mr. Guilmartin's yard was laid out with an enticing array of antiques and other intriguing items. Among them were little witches' broomsticks. We bought a set of 3 for a dollar.

Frank Pannenborg, my father's college friend, was visiting with us that day. He likes to see people's projects, so when I made my first witch, Mallory, I e-mailed him a photograph. He replied with a bit of character background on her, saying "She's a very sweet witch – probably had a hard time socially in Witch School." She did come out with a slightly anxious facial expression.

With that, an idea began to form in my mind: why not have fun making more dolls? I could create 3 witches, improve my sewing skills, and finally figure out how to make beautiful, comfortable dresses with pockets…in miniature.

Antoinette had been built up in my imagination over the past couple of decades – maybe even longer. For her, I sent Frank some details on her character background. She was mine to fill out the back-story of!

From there, I was off, creating more characters.

The character of Lilith began as a witch, and evolved into a more complex one rather quickly, as I added more details and skills to her.

The alien, Ileandra, was taken from a novel I wrote during the pandemic. She returned for another novel, and it was a thrill to bring her to life as a doll.

It soon became something that I looked forward to doing as often as I could. Once I had used up most of the rectangles of fabric left over from making masks during the pandemic, I loved to find beautiful fabrics online.

The fabrics came from Joann, Etsy, Amazon, and Spoonflower.

Spoonflower is a fascinating source of material because artists from all over the planet upload their patterns to its website, carefully configured to repeat seamlessly once printed onto whatever variety of cloth is desired. I learned what it is like to work with cotton poplin, cotton jersey, cotton lawn, and petal signature cotton. Each one has a different feel to it.

The artists whose designs appear on the Spoonflower website make some gorgeous images, and some fascinating ones. My favorite is Utart, but others that I like are Thistle and Fox, Rachel Quinlan, Weaving Major, M to the Fifth Power, Simone Balman, 3rittanyLane, Peacoquette Designs, Chelsea Rockey Graphic Design, Hip Kid Designs, Charlotte Winter, Flowers for Bear, AngelGer28, and Coffee and Pixels.

On Etsy, a brand of fabric called Timeless Treasures makes the most wonderfully soft cotton in a fascinating and beautiful array of patterns.

Designing the outfits was a lot of fun. Sometimes I learned by accident how to make an element of a dress that I had liked. Other times, I watched a YouTube video to learn a technique. Staring at images on Pinterest helped, too.

The next part of my addictive routine was photographing the dolls in each outfit.

I have enjoyed it all to the point that I was sorry to finish this project.

Details about the Dolls

Each of these dolls has her names written in Chancery Italic calligraphy on her left ankle.

Their faces, ears, earrings, and manicures were stitched with cotton stranded mouliné embroidery threads.

Their hair came from American Girl Doll wigs, sewn onto their heads.

Lilith
Hermione
Wandcraft

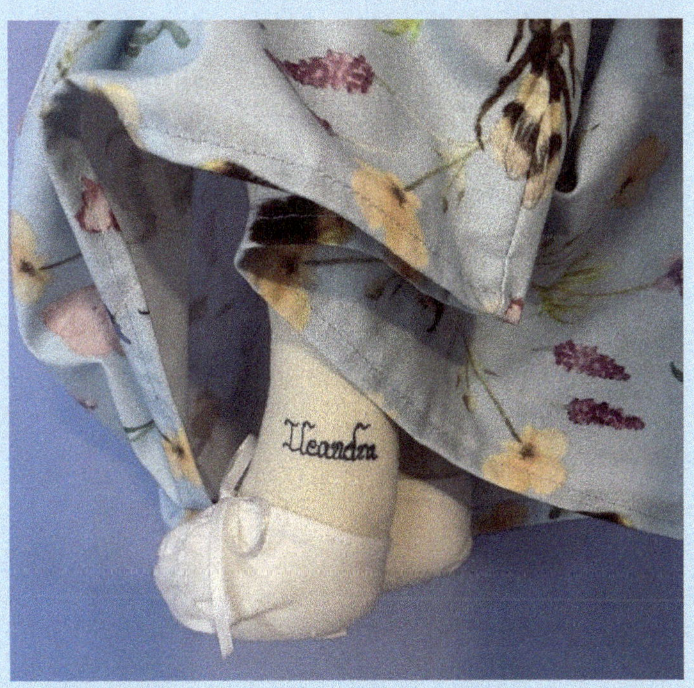
Ileandra

About the Dessert Photographs

The photographs of desserts that appear in this book are my own.

I love to bake – to make a work of edible art out of a dessert – and then to memorialize my creation in a photograph before cutting into it and eating it.

Recipes include ones that I love from cookbooks, plus some that I have tweaked just for the fun of it to make them unique and with a different flavor.

Some recipes are even ones that I created myself.

It's part of the fun of life to make these things and spoil the people I care about with delectable desserts.

Acknowledgements

There are some people I have to thank for making this book a reality.

My father gave me a Nikon camera and taught me how to use it.

My grandmother, Anna Ruth Baker Fox taught me how to sew when I was eleven years old.

My Aunt Joan Fox, an artist who studied at the Rhode Island School of Design, was happy to offer encouragement and view dress after dress.

My mother bought me a sewing machine during the pandemic, which got me started sewing. She was endless fun to discuss this project with and show the dolls to in their dresses, and to bounce ideas off of. She also encouraged me and steered me as I embroidered Ileandra's eyes, to make sure that they looked as they should. We were both pleased with the result. My mother found this project exciting as she watched each doll brought down the runway to be viewed. She also edited the manuscript, because no author can find their own errors! Thank you, Mommy!

My uncle, Douglas A. Conant, and my friend, Adam M. Frost of computercareandlearning (he is not a fan of capital letters!), taught me most of what I know about using a computer.

All of these people enabled me to create the dolls and this book, and it was a thrill to bring all of these parts of my life together.

About the Author

Stephanie C. Fox, J.D. is a historian, writer, and editor. She is a graduate of William Smith College and of the University of Connecticut School of Law.

She runs an editing service called *QueenBeeEdit*, which caters to politicians, scientists, and others, which can be accessed at
https://www.queenbeeedit.com.

Her imprint is *QueenBeeBooks*. Her shop on Etsy, for doll clothing, is *QueenBeeCouturière*, found at
https://queenbeecouturiere.etsy.com

Stephanie lives in Connecticut, and has written books about a variety of topics, including Asperger's, the global financial meltdown, honey bee colony collapse disorder, travelogues of a trips to Kuwait and Hawai'i, the effects of human overpopulation on the environment, and cats.

The Author with Her Dolls

After a few months of sewing, I realized that I knew enough to be able to make clothing for humans.

Actually, I had a jumper from a crafts fair that still fit; I will convert it to a skirt and use the top for more doll clothing at some point. But I found fabric on Etsy with the same pattern (black background to my jumper's white one), and got the fun idea of posing with Antoinette in our matching outfits.

Then I decided to make a few blouses, and got fabric from Spoonflower to match some of my favorite dresses for Lilith and Ileandra.

By this point, I dared to risk making something for my aunt: a shirt with chickadees on it – her favorite bird which, she told me, sings a summer and a winter tune. She was thrilled with her surprise gift.

That left a little bit of fabric from top to bottom of each yard of it, which was enough for a few more doll shirts.

So, I had just a little bit more fun making doll clothing for this project.

If you want me to make a dress for your doll, please visit my doll shop on Etsy at
https://queenbeecouturiere.etsy.com

Antoinette and Stephanie

Raspberries and Blossoms Pattern

Lilith and Stephanie

Dragonfly Garden Pattern

Ileandra and Stephanie

Watercolor Bees and Flowers Pattern